TANGLES

by
ERROL BROOME

illustrated
by
ANN JAMES

A TRUMPET CLUB SPECIAL EDITION

Published by The Trumpet Club, Inc., a subsidiary of
Bantam Doubleday Dell Publishing Group, Inc., 1540 Broadway, New York,
New York 10036. "A Trumpet Club Special Edition" with the portrayal of a
trumpet and two circles is a registered trademark of
Bantam Doubleday Dell Publishing Group, Inc.

Text copyright © 1993 by Errol Broome
Illustrations copyright © 1993 by Ann James
Cover illustration copyright © 1994 by Pamela Patrick

ISBN 0-440-83586-0

This edition published by arrangement with Alfred A. Knopf, Inc.,
a division of Random House, Inc.

Printed in the United States of America
May 1996
1 3 5 7 9 10 8 6 4 2
OPM

To everything there is a season...

ONE

F IT HADN'T BEEN for the car, none of this would have happened.

There was a screech of brakes, then nothing. A moment's silence. A car door slammed. Dad went out to have a look.

Mum and I went to the kitchen window. Tom sat at the table and asked when were we going to have dinner, anyway. Then Dad stuck his head around the back gate and yelled: "Don't come out here! Stay inside!"

It was getting dark, but when the gate opened again I saw Dad with something in his arms. It was Ginger. Dad carried him across his hands, gently, like a parcel. I knew straight away that Ginger was dead.

We buried him under the laurel tree. Dad took off his hat and dug a hole. We stood around in the dark, and afterwards I sprinkled rose petals on the mound. They all said they were sorry. Even Tom.

I'd seen it, I knew it, but I didn't believe Ginger had gone till I went to bed that night. There was no warm lump on the end of my bed. In the morning, there was no scratching on the carpet when he asked to go outside.

I didn't say a word at breakfast. Nobody said much. Dad made a huge pile of toast. He just kept on making it.

"You know, Sophie," he said, "that poor man was nearly as upset about this as you are."

I stared at the pile of toast and didn't take any.

"He even offered to buy you another cat."

"What did you say?" asked Mum.

"I told him not to worry about it."

"Maybe one day," said Mum.

"No," said Tom. "What about my pigeons?"

Their voices came to me as if they were in another room. I heard myself answer. "I don't want one anyway. I'll never want another cat."

"You'll change your mind," said Dad.

I kept seeing Ginger, lying dead across Dad's arms. How could you get that out of your mind?

"I don't think so," I said.

After school, Mrs. Cochran invited me in for tea. I heard her dog, Watson, scruffing around next door, and then she yelled out from behind the fence. "Are you there, Sophie? There are cookies!"

That meant warm cookies, fresh from the

oven. I'm not stupid, and I knew she'd baked them for me. She thought food would take my mind off other things. It wouldn't. But I said yes anyway.

The first things you see at Mrs. Cochran's house are forget-me-nots growing in the door-mat. The mat is falling to bits. It's held together with dirt and stuff from people's shoes. Every day, Mrs. Cochran sits on the doorstep and picks seeds out of her stockings.

That afternoon, I followed her thick brown stockings in thick brown shoes down the path around the side of the house. Creepers tugged at my hair. Watson lay like a black sack on the bricks. His jowl sagged. Slobber hung from his mouth. Poor old Watson—he looked about a hundred.

Every morning, he tottered behind Mrs. Cochran when she walked to the corner shop. Tom reckoned poor old Watson couldn't keep up with a tortoise.

I gave him a pat on the ears. Mrs. Cochran was lucky to have a dog, even an old one. In my head I heard that screech of brakes, again and again, as loud as the night before. I trailed behind Mrs. Cochran to the messy part of the garden. She calls it The Wild. It's always different, like someone who throws their clothes on the floor each night and puts on new ones the next day.

The bluebells of last week had gone,

and daisies were pushing above everything. The white-and-yellow heads were fresh, even though Ginger was dead. I stared at their bright faces. Nothing stopped for Ginger, except me.

Mrs. Cochran put her arm round my shoulder.

"They're cheeky things, daisies. They won't wait their turn."

We walked down the path, and she knew what I was thinking. "The bluebells will come again next year," she said, but it seemed a long time till then.

She snipped some daisies and a geranium, forget-me-nots, pansies, pinks. I know them all now.

By the time we had walked back to the

house, she'd made them into a posy. Posies are for taking home to Mum. "But this one's for you," she said.

She poured tea into blue-and-white cups and served the cookies in a table napkin. Poor old Watson dragged open the screen door and flopped on the floor beside her chair. I looked at him and wished he was Ginger.

I wasn't hungry. I hooked my feet around the legs of the chair and took the nearest cookie, to be polite. Mrs. Cochran talked like a kettle always on the boil. Bubbles of laughter spurted across the kitchen.

"I heard the first cicadas at 8:17 last night," she said.

I looked up. "Exactly?"

"Exactly."

"I heard them, too."

"I knew you would." She patted my hand.

"You and I hear the same things, Sophie."

Mrs. Cochran never stood still. Her thin stick legs darted from one place to another while she tipped water into potted plants on the shelves.

"It's the hospital fair next month," she said. "I'm working on the plant booth again. Helped with the cakes for years, but I'm really much better at plants. Have another cookie, dear."

I couldn't fit one in. I picked up the posy from the table. "But I'll come again tomorrow."

I knew I'd be needing Mrs. Cochran.

I heard Mum and Tom in the kitchen.

"Where's Sophie?" asked Mum.

"In her room," said Tom. "She's always in her room."

"What's she doing in there?"

"Nothing, I bet. At least she could help with the pigeons."

"Good idea!" Mum was on her way. She

opened the door of my room. I was kneeling on the bed, looking out the window.

"Come on, Sophie, stop mooning. Tom's taking Speckle and Spot to the park. He could do with a hand."

I swung my legs over the side of the bed and sat there, staring at the wall. "I don't feel like it."

Only eight days, and everybody had forgotten about Ginger. Eight days! Did they expect me to chase after stupid pigeons, as if nothing had happened?

I knew Mum was trying to get me out of the bedroom. What's wrong with being in your bedroom when you want to be alone?

"Steve and Billy will be down there," I said. "Billy *loves* homing pigeons."

"Very well." Mum spoke in her tight, hurt voice. Her hair hung over her face, like it did when she was fed up. "But *I* could do with a hand, too. It's only a week to the fair, you know. We need heaps more for the gift booth."

They all kept talking about the fair. Couldn't they think of anything else? Well, they could leave me out of it. I wouldn't be going this year.

TWO

"WHAT-HO, SOPHIE! Your silkworms have hatched!" Dad was rummaging among his hats when he found them. "Quick! Look at the poor things. We must get some mulberry leaves." He handed down the open shoebox.

"Help!" I said. "They're alive!" Tiny black threads waved among the old eggs. Every winter, I forgot them. The year before, they hatched and starved to death in the cupboard. I felt bad for a few days and then cadged silkworms from friends at school.

Sometimes I wondered why I bothered with them. Nine months out of the year, they were stuffed away in a cupboard. But every spring—like now—I started over again.

"Don't just stand there," said Dad. "We don't know how long ago these things hatched. Now, which hat will I wear today?"

Dad has hats. When we were little, he wore a different one each day, to surprise us. Sometimes he wore a police hat or a soldier's helmet, to make us laugh. Once he wore a clown's cap. Friends heard about his hats and gave him their old ones. Now we had a cupboard full. That day, he picked his gray felt hat to wear to work.

I put the shoebox on the kitchen table. "I'll ask Mrs. Cochran if I can pick her mulberry leaves again."

Mrs. Cochran was repotting herbs. Poor old Watson flopped beside the wheelbarrow.

"The silkworms are in again, are they?" She pointed the way to the mulberry tree.

There were no cookies that afternoon. But there was a frog in the fountain and an enormous brown snail. Mrs. Cochran pulled it from the soil, with a white glug of eggs stuck to it. I didn't know that snails laid eggs.

She clucked as if she was sorry, then squashed it under her shoe. "Can't let it eat my daffodils!"

I looked away and then ran to the mulberry tree. Tiny pale shoots were coming on almost bare branches.

"You know where to find the tree," said Mrs. Cochran. "Come in whenever you like. Don't bother to ask."

Most afternoons, I walked home from school

with Carla. I asked if she wanted to see my silk-worms.

"They've hatched."

She crinkled her nose in a way that said "Not really, but I'll come if you want me to."

I did want her to. Carla listens when you tell her things. She's never in a hurry. When we buy ice-creams, I bite and Carla licks, so hers lasts all the way home.

Carla's hair is black and sometimes shines all silvery. She's calm, too, like the river when there's no wind. I wish I could be like that, and not have a mouth that says stupid things and a face that goes red when people look at me.

And another thing: Carla's mother goes for picnics. I'd like a mother like Mrs. Maccari, who takes you for picnics on Sundays.

"Will your Mum be there?" asked Carla.

"Yes."

"Your Mum's always there when you get home."

"Yes." I didn't say that she's always in the shed, making pots. If she isn't on duty at the hospital, she's off at some market every weekend, selling her pots.

I thought maybe we could swap mothers for a while. But I knew I was stuck with Mum. Dad would never go on picnics with Mrs. Maccari.

Carla held her head on one side, like she does when she's thinking. "You've got a brother, too," she said.

People who haven't got brothers always wish they had one.

"Cats are better," I said, and felt alone again.

Carla looked at me sideways, as if she wasn't really looking. "Cats are good, too, but you had a special one."

I didn't want to talk about it.

I stared ahead and walked more quickly. Carla didn't say anything until we reached our house. "It'll be all right," she said gently, as we opened the gate.

"Do you want to come to Mrs. Cochran's first, to get mulberry leaves?" I asked.

Carla said yes.

I'm lucky to have a friend like Carla.

That day, Mrs. Cochran had burnt-butter

biscuits, and two ducks to eat the snails.

Carla sat at the table and stared at the clutter. You never feel cold in Mrs. Cochran's kitchen.

Poor old Watson snored beside the stove.

"We've only got a parakeet at our place," said Carla. "He doesn't even talk."

"Who does?" said Mrs. Cochran. She stuffed wisps of hair into the bun at the back of her neck. "Watson doesn't talk. The quackers out there don't talk. Tom's pigeons don't talk. Why should a poor old parakeet have to talk?"

Ginger didn't talk, either. But he nearly did. I understood him. At school that day, someone had asked, "Are you going to get another cat?"—when Ginger had been dead only thirteen days! How could you bury Ginger and take in another cat, like buying a new pair of sneakers? Throw out one lot, get another, everything's okay. Well, not with me, it isn't.

"You're very quiet today, Sophie." Mrs.

Cochran jumped from her chair. "Let's go and pick the leaves and see what else we can find out there."

We were knee-deep in The Wild when the ducks scrabbled towards us. Their bills snapped open and shut. Carla laughed and held out her hands to them. "What a funny noise!"

It was an ugly noise. I tried to like the ducks, but there was a hole inside me they couldn't take away.

"We might get an egg or two," said Mrs. Cochran.

"And ducklings?" asked Carla.

Mrs. Cochran held up her arms. "Two's enough!"

The ducks nosed off into the grass.

Carla stood and gazed at the white waves of daisies. Her own backyard had rows and rows of vegetables. She was in no hurry to leave Mrs. Cochran's place.

Mrs. Cochran smiled at me and whispered that down among the milkweed there would soon be butterflies.

Just then, we heard voices from next door in our pigeon coop.

"Tom's home," said Carla.

"And Steve." He's a friend. "They'll be taking the pigeons down to the park. Tom's going to race them soon."

"Can we go and look?"

I said they were only pigeons, but we'd go if she wanted to see them.

It's a five-minute walk to the park. Two bicycles lay together near the goalposts. Out in the center, Tom and Steve were playing cricket. Tom waved his bat at us. "Don't open the box!" he yelled.

As if I would! I pulled off my shoes and threw them on the grass. "Here comes Billy Winks." Billy was always hanging around.

He jumped off his bicycle and left it on the grass with the wheels still spinning. "Hi!" he puffed and ran off to join the boys. "What are you doing?"

"What does it look like we're doing?" said Tom.

"When are you going to let the pigeons out?"

"When we feel like it."

"Can I have a bowl?"

Steve threw the ball to Billy and called out to us. "Want a bat?"

I like cricket. I'm not bad at it either. I pulled Carla by the arm.

She pulled back. "You go on, I'll field." Carla would rather sit under a tree and watch. Or read a book or write a story. She's always writing stories.

Carla stood on the boundary while Billy jigged in to bowl to me. His stringy bangs bobbed up and down. He's a bit of a joke, Billy, but you can't help liking him. Well, I like him. Tom thinks he's a pest.

Billy flicked the ball from his fist and grunted with the effort. I pulled back the bat and whacked the ball. I never know where it will go, but this one shot across the grass and right through Carla's legs. I heard Steve mutter as it headed into the trees.

"I'm sick of this," said Tom, when we'd only just started. "Let's release the pigeons."

"When are you going to take them further away?" asked Billy.

"Dunno," said Tom. "Depends."

"How do they know the way back to your place?"

Tom clamped the cricket bat on the carrier of his bicycle. "Dunno."

"Nobody knows." I tried to make up for Tom's crummy answers. "It's like magic."

"We should put the coop on the roof, though," said Tom.

"You need a fantail pigeon," said Steve. "Uncle Vince's got a fantail. They're good. They hang around the place, so the homers know when they're home."

"Yeah, I could do with a fantail."

"They're beautiful," said Carla.

"Why don't you get a fantail, then?" asked Billy.

"Can't afford it. Don't think I'll ever get one."

"How much does it cost, a fantail?"

"I don't know, Billy." Tom sighed as loudly as he could. "Have you got any other questions?"

Billy shook his head. "They might have one at the fair. Are you going to the fair?"

"'Course we are. Never seen a fantail there, though." He bent down and unhooked the lid of the box. "Now, get ready to ride!" The two speckled pigeons flew out of the box. They flapped around our heads, then circled away from the park.

Tom dumped the box across the handlebars. "Come on, let's go."

"Beat 'em home!" sang Billy. "Beat 'em home!" He jerked the front wheel of his bicycle as he pedaled faster and faster behind the others.

"I hope they're all right," said Carla.

"Who? The boys or the pigeons?"

"The pigeons, of course."

I started to do up my shoelaces. I stood on one leg and then the other, as I tied them. "Pigeons are boring," I said. "I'd rather have a cat."

"You said you'd never have another cat."

"Well…well, I won't."

"It was awful, Ginger dying like that, for no reason."

"He wasn't even old," I said.

We began to walk along the footpath. "How old's your mother?" asked Carla.

"I don't know. Why?"

"Mine's old. You're lucky, your mother's young."

"How do you know?" I climbed onto a wall and edged along the top while Carla walked below.

"I can tell. My mother sits down to do up her shoelaces. She used to tie them with her feet in the air, like you do."

I held out my arms to keep my balance on the wall. Ginger could have walked on the highest fence without a single wobble. "Mum can still do a split."

"See, I told you."

I didn't look down. "She goes up the stairs two at a time, too."

Carla breathed a slow, soft sigh. "I don't want my mother to be old." Carla is always thinking about things.

"She's ahead of my mum, that's all," I said. I came to the end of the wall. A tree between houses blocked the way, with its branches hanging over the footpath. I jumped to the ground. "Hey, it's a mulberry tree!" I was glad Mrs. Cochran had a tree and I didn't need to come this far to collect mulberry leaves.

We walked home the short way, down Stringers Lane. Well, Carla glided while I walked. And she didn't once step on a crack.

THREE

"GET UP, SOPHIE, we'll be late for the fair."

I rolled over, but didn't open my eyes. The blanket felt light, and there was no warm patch where Ginger would have been. "I'm not coming."

"Not coming? Rubbish!" said Tom. "What are you going to do all day?"

"Go away. I'll be all right."

I heard Tom's foot hit the squeaky board in the passage and knew he was near the kitchen door.

"She says she's not coming."

"Rubbish!" said Mum.

"That's what I said."

"Tell her Dad needs her help with the white elephants. It's about time she did something."

She's pretending, I thought. There wouldn't be white elephants at the hospital fair. No elephants at all. But it sounded interesting. I opened my eyes and stared at the dull green wall and the silkworm box on the floor. I'd be alone with the silkworms all day.

I walked barefoot down the passage and stood at the kitchen door. "What do you mean...white elephants?"

"A load of old junk," said Dad. He had three hats on the table.

"Tell me really."

He had a mouthful of toast and honey. "You'd be surprised, sometimes."

"Can I come?" The words slipped out.

"You're coming!" said Dad. Honey dripped down his chin. He reached into his pocket and pulled out his wallet. "Here! Five dollars each for you and Tom, and that's it; no more. Don't waste it."

The hospital is about five miles from our place. The park next to it is mostly quiet, but it was like a funfair that morning. Parked cars lined the streets. People jammed through the gates. Everyone in Cattlesea was there.

I followed Dad's Mexican hat, past stacks of dusty old books, past the merry-go-round and puffs of pink cotton candy.

"Here we are," said Dad.

"Where?"

"The white elephant booth."

He had to be joking! I looked around at the big muddle of junk. There wasn't an elephant in sight. Not one, as far as I could see. Dad leaned against an old refrigerator and talked to Mr. Speers from Grant Street. Around them on the ground were six or seven television sets, thin carpets, curtains, car tires, lampshades, and a canary cage. There were trestle tables covered with things grannies keep on mantelpieces. There were china animals and vases and hairpins and beads.

"Is that all it is?"

"All what is?"

"A white elephant booth."

Dad laughed. "What else do you want? Looks as if it's all here."

I knew I shouldn't have gone to the fair. "You mean it's all junk—old things that nobody wants?"

Dad jerked his head toward buyers sifting through the jewelry. "Funny thing, Sophie, is that there's always someone who *does* want it."

He went across to serve them.

I still don't know why anyone wants a lumpy mattress or a pram without a wheel, but when I started looking at things, they weren't so bad after all. I found a carved wooden box with the catch missing.

"It's had its day," said Dad.

Still, I liked it and I bought it. Then I saw a necklace made of shells and a glass candlestick for two dollars, so I bought them too.

I skipped between booths, counting my money in my head. Mum and Dad's friends kept saying hello, and I bet they were thinking: "Sophie's happy today." Well, I *was* nearly happy. I wished Carla would finish her music lesson, so we could ride the Horror Scope.

I bought a sample bag that was half full of things like pencils and plastic rulers and really, really old comics. Then I had to buy a hamburger. I couldn't walk past the smell. I sat on a bench to eat it, but even then I was thinking of Ginger. I could hear his miaow inside my head and I didn't know how I'd ever forget it.

There it was again, so clear you'd have thought it was here, at the fair. *Miaow*. It couldn't be Ginger. He'd never come back. But something was calling through the noise of the carnival. Definitely something. I stumbled through the crowd. I followed the sound, because I knew I wasn't imagining it. Ahead, a group of children huddled around the surprise booth. They were peering into a box. A sign on the box said: $5.00 each.

Kittens!

I touched the black one on the head. It gave me a sandpaper lick. I wanted it to be mine. I opened my purse, quickly, before the other kids beat me to it. One dollar. One measly dollar.

That stupid sample bag! Why did I have to buy it?

I stood there, with my purse open, and a ripped-out, empty feeling in my stomach. The sample bag lay on the ground between my feet. I didn't want a thing in it. "Please," I said to a woman who was working at the booth. "Please could you keep the black one for me?"

She gave me a funny look.

"I'll get the money. I need more."

She smiled. "I'll keep it till 12 o'clock. I'll put your name on it!"

I ran to the gift booth. "Mum! Mum, can I have four dollars to buy a kitten?"

"A kitten?" Mum didn't know whether to look pleased or not so pleased.

"I need four dollars."

She looked at me, but not with her eyes, like she does when she's got other things on her mind. "I thought Dad gave you five dollars—I can't think about this now, Sophie. Can't you see I'm busy?"

"Mum, please, it's there…waiting for me."

Mum put an apron in a paper bag. Aprons, aprons everywhere. Who cared about aprons! We had them hanging behind the kitchen door and no one ever wore them. I pushed in front of a girl who was trying on a sunhat. "Mum, I need it *now*. I'll pay you back."

People were waiting to be served. Mum was starting to worry about them. "Look, Sophie, we have to talk about things like this. Come back and see me later." She turned to the girl with the sunhat. "I'm sorry to keep you waiting."

"Then it will be too late," I muttered. She didn't even hear me. I decided to go and ask Dad. He'd help me. I couldn't let the kitten go, not now I'd seen it. Dad would give me the money.

I ran all the way to the white elephant stall. "Dad! Dad, can I have four dollars to buy a kitten?"

"Hold it! Hold it!" Dad put up his arm, like a traffic officer. "What's this all about?"

"I need four dollars—only four. There's kittens."

"Kittens, eh?" He pushed back his Mexican hat.

"And I need the money."

"I gave you five dollars. You should have thought about it before you wasted your money on junk."

"Da-ad!"

"Don't try that on me, Sophie. I'm busy!" He

turned to another man. "Can I help you?"

Not Dad, too. I felt sick inside. There was a horrid, sweet taste in my mouth. I stumbled into the crowd. I had to find Tom—he was my only chance now. He and Steve would be at the darts. Tom liked to win money, and he was good at darts.

He was with Steve and Fritz Bolton, and Billy was there too. They were standing around as if the stall was their private property.

"Hi, bubblegum legs," called Steve. You'd think he'd never seen pink tights before.

"Tom, can you lend me four dollars?"

"Whoa, there, Sis. What for?"

"For a kitten. I want to buy a kitten."

"*I* don't want to buy a kitten."

"It'll be mine. Please, Tom, I'll pay you back."

"I've heard that before. Where's your money gone?"

"I bought some things—and then I saw this kitten. It's jammed up in a box with people prodding it. Please, Tom, please."

Fritz jabbed Tom in the back. "C'mon, let's get going."

"Why don't you have a go at the darts?" said Tom. "You might *win* yourself a kitten."

Tom knew I was no good at darts. "Would you throw for me?" I asked.

"What? You pay the money and I throw the darts?"

I nodded and gave the man my last dollar.

"Sounds okay to me." Tom took the darts. "One kitten coming up."

"Call him Ace, eh?" said Steve.

"Call him Dart," said Billy.

"Call him a pest," said Fritz. "We gotta get going."

"All right, hang on," said Tom. He threw the darts quickly, one after the other like shots from a pistol. "There you go. A dollar back already!"

"But I need more," I whispered.

"*You* have a shot, then. I've got to go."

"But, Tom…"

They all walked off. "Hope you get it," said Billy, and I stood there, knowing I had no chance. The fair was over for me. People pushed past me, and I didn't see any of them.

I began to run. I'd go and sit in the car. I'd sit there until this horrid fair was over. I ran and ran and could hardly see where I was going.

"Sophie, you *are* in a hurry!"

I stopped and saw Mrs. Cochran's brown shoes on the grass. I looked up.

"Why, Sophie, whatever's wrong?"

"Nothing. I'm going home."

"So soon?" Mrs. Cochran's face smiled above her box of potted plants. "When I'm only just arriving?"

"I've got to go," I said. I knew I should help

Mrs. Cochran to carry the pots across the park. I knew I should stay till Carla arrived. I knew lots of things and wished it was all different.

I watched Mrs. Cochran walk slowly through the crowd. The box tilted and something slipped to the ground. I walked back to pick it up. It was a brown leather wallet. I held it out, but Mrs. Cochran had moved out of sight.

I only needed to run after her and ask for the money. But I couldn't be sure she'd lend it to me. Could I risk losing it, now that I had it—right here?

The wallet felt heavy in my hand. I turned and ran to the bathroom.

Safe inside, I bolted the door and opened the wallet. It was not very thick, but I saw some red notes and…a purple five-dollar note. I tugged it out. Five dollars! A kitten!

The woman at the surprise booth would be wondering whether I was coming. Five dollars was all I needed. Mrs. Cochran might not notice if five dollars was missing. Only five dollars. I'd leave the rest.

I put the five-dollar note in my purse. Now I'd return the wallet to Mrs. Cochran at the plant booth. But I couldn't. What if she knew the money was missing? She *would* know. Then what?

I thought I could leave the wallet there, on a shelf in the bathroom. Someone would hand it in. Nobody would know how it got there or who had taken the five dollars. But someone might steal the wallet. Steal it! A thief!

A pain like a knife stabbed at my chest. *I'm* a thief. No! No! I hadn't *taken* the wallet. I'd only picked it up and taken what I needed. I *do* need it. Well, I *want* it. I really want it. And I've borrowed it, that's all. I was arguing with myself, and it was like a tennis match in my head. The ball went backwards and forwards, and I had to keep on hitting it. I couldn't stop myself. I *had* to have the money. It was too late now to ask. I'd taken it.

I ran to the fair office. Nobody saw me. I'm sure nobody saw me. I put the wallet on the counter and ran away. I ran and ran and could hardly breathe when I reached the surprise booth. I could see the box. What if the kitten had gone? What if someone else had taken it?

Maybe I was already being punished for what I had done. I walked the last few steps and looked into the box.

The kitten lay like a ball of black wool, all in a tangle. One back leg curled underneath him. The other strung out behind. His front paws were crossed over his face, so that only his eyes looked up at me from a corner of the box.

"Ah, you've come for your kitten. He's the last one, so you can take him in the box."

I gave the money to the woman and walked away with my head almost inside the box. The kitten stretched and shook and rolled to one side.

"Oops. Tangles," I said, and after that I couldn't call him anything else.

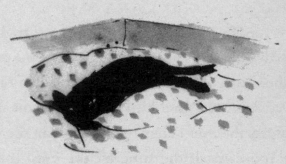

FOUR

LET ME TELL YOU now that Tangles has gold-green eyes and fur as black as you can get. There isn't a scrap of any other color on him. Dad says we'll lose him one dark night, but he forgets the eyes. They're like lights in the dark.

You can tell the time by the eyes; that's the first thing you notice when you have a cat. At night, they let in the light and grow huge and round and shining. In the daytime, the pupils get thinner and thinner, until by lunchtime, they're slits, as thin as a thread of hair.

So, around seven o'clock by Tangles' eyes, Tom came home from the fair. I was in my room with Tangles, and it was peaceful; just him and me getting to know each other. It was nearly perfect, except for a feeling like an ache inside, a feeling that it would not always be like this.

I heard Tom in the kitchen with Mum, and then he stuck his head around the door of my room. "You did it, Soph! Good on you! Knew you could!"

I smiled, but words wouldn't come. My throat dried up. I sat on the bed and held Tangles out to him. He rubbed his fingers under Tangles' chin. "How'd you do it, eh?"

"I just did."

I could tell he liked Tangles. He said a new cat was all right with him, as long as I trained it not to chase his pigeons.

Everyone was happy that night. Dad came in, with his Mexican hat pushed back to make room for his smile. "What-ho, Sophie!" he said. "We sold everything. Someone even wanted to buy my hat." He peered at the kitten. "And what have we got here?"

"Good old Sophie," said Tom. "She's a hotshot at darts, now."

I gave a sort of smile and looked at the floor. There were some things I didn't want to talk about, ever again.

Carla heard about the kitten and came around the next morning. Everyone was pleased that I'd stopped being miserable, and I didn't tell them I had a stomach ache.

Carla and I made a box for Tangles, with a mat and a cushion. Then we took him into the garden to play. He wanted to explore everything. He pushed his nose against the wire of the pigeon coop and tried to climb the wattle tree. For a moment, I looked for Ginger among the branches.

Poor old Watson coughed out a tired bark when Tangles nosed too close to Mrs. Cochran's fence.

"Let's go in and get some mulberry leaves," said Carla.

"Not today. I'd rather stay here."

"But you haven't fed your silkworms today."

"They're all right," I said. "Don't boss me around."

Carla didn't say anything. She looked a bit shocked, though. Carla had never bossed anyone around in her life. She stayed with me in the garden, and we talked and played with Tangles and watched Tom clean out the pigeon coop.

Then Billy turned up.

He came bouncing in with this cardboard box and handed it to Tom. "It's for you."

Tom opened the box and a snow-white fantail pigeon flew into the coop. "Hey, it's a beauty!" he said. "Where'd you get it?"

"I bought it," said Billy. "It's a present." He had this dopey grin on his face, as if he'd just won a prize or something.

Tom kept on staring at the fantail. "Aw, Billy, you shouldn't've."

And Billy kept on smiling. "Glad you like it. You need a fantail when you're racing."

Tangles ran across to the coop and stopped just short of the wire. His tail stuck up in the air, and the hair rose along his back. His body arched, until he stood there like a hairpin, hissing at the new white bird.

Carla laughed. "He's only been here a day, and he acts as if he owns the place."

I wanted Tangles to own the place. I wanted to know that he would always be here. I knew, too, that I'd be dead meat if Tangles attacked the fantail. I'd have to get him used to the new bird. Once it was at home in our coop, it would strut around the yard as if it were boss of the place.

It was a beautiful bird. I hoped Tom would be nicer to Billy after this.

Tangles soon found the best furniture. He sharpened his claws on the armchair and tried to climb the sitting-room curtains. Mum said she could do without all this again, but she didn't mind, really.

Dad said: "Tell you what, I'll give you a new chair for your birthday."

Mum didn't look too keen, but she said it would be nice.

47

So, etimes Mrs. Cochran called over the fence. I talked to her through the crack, where I couldn't see her face properly. I couldn't see The Wild, either, but I knew that poppies would be splashing through the long grass, as if someone had spilled a box of paints.

"You haven't been in for weeks," she said. "I want to see that new kitten—and what about your silkworms?"

"They're all right. I…I found a mulberry tree up the street."

"You can come in here anytime, Sophie."

"I know, but…but this is a big tree. It doesn't matter if I pick the leaves."

"It doesn't matter a scrap if you pick the leaves on my tree," said Mrs. Cochran. I wished she'd stop. "And besides, I like to see you."

"Yes." I knew that. I liked to see her too. I *wanted* to see her. "I'll come in soon," I said. But

I didn't. I went on picking leaves from the tree near Stringers Lane.

"Where are you going?" Mum asked one afternoon.

"Nowhere."

"You're not going nowhere without telling me."

"Anywhere!"

"Don't be irritating, either, Sophie. I know perfectly well how to speak." She grew hot and cross. "You really *are* irritating. I don't know what's got into you lately."

"Nothing," I said. "And if you want to know, I'm just going to pick mulberry leaves from a tree that's better than Mrs. Cochran's tree. So there!"

On days like this, I didn't like what was happening to me. But no matter how much I thought about it, I couldn't help the things I said and did.

FIVE

TANGLES CURLED ON my lap when I did my homework. Sometimes he climbed on my shoulder and jabbed his claws through my sweatshirt. I used to carry Ginger that way, around my neck like a scarf or one of those foxes with their heads still on that grandmothers wore in the olden days. Pene Schmidt's got one in her dress-up box. It gives you the creeps a bit.

Ginger had been warm and soft across my shoulders.

Tangles climbed trees, too, and liked the same big one that Ginger used to climb. Its branches hung over Mrs. Cochran's fence. She saw Tangles one day and called out, "Hello, kitten," and Watson gave a few weak barks. I called Tangles down, but he wouldn't come.

"He's grown," Mrs. Cochran called through the fence.

I waited, thinking what to say. I knew she was standing in a clump of wild carrots, with flowers like white lace handkerchiefs.

"It's a very long time since you've been over, Sophie."

"I've been busy." I wondered what new things Mrs. Cochran had since last time I was there.

"Yes, yes. And how are the silkworms?"

"Spinning. Most of them are starting to spin."

"Perhaps you'll come in tomorrow?"

I didn't answer. I wished Tangles would come down from the tree, but he stayed there, tapping and scratching, and stared down with eyes that said five o'clock. Pigeons flew around his head and didn't bother him at all.

"All right, stay there!" I said, and went inside.

It was just my luck to walk into Tom and Steve. "We're going to have a game of darts," they said.

Darts! I didn't want to have anything more to do with darts.

They hung the dartboard on the wall at the end of the veranda. They were just starting the game when we heard the crash of a bicycle against the side of the house.

"Billy!" said Tom.

Billy ran onto the veranda, like someone's pet puppy. "What're you doing?"

Tom and Steve didn't answer. Tom never does if he thinks you should know the answer, and I mean they *did* look as though they were playing darts.

"They're playing darts," I said.

"Can I play?"

Tom looked at Steve. I could see he was thinking of the fantail Billy had given him.

"Well, okay. How about Steve and me on to you and Sophie? She can show us how good she is."

"No," I said. "Billy and I want to feed the pigeons."

"That's all right," said Billy. "We can do that later. We'll play darts now."

Billy always does what Tom wants him to do.

"I'd rather feed pigeons," I said.

"Bad luck! Billy'd rather play darts. What's wrong with you, Sophie? You can show us how you did it."

Everyone kept asking what was wrong with me, and I couldn't explain. If I could, I couldn't tell them. It was like having a hole in your jeans that keeps getting bigger and bigger.

"I don't like beating you, that's all." I tried to make a joke of it, and after a while they gave up. I'd managed to get out of that one. But I wondered what would be next.

I didn't have long to wait. Mum was in the middle of making fudge pudding when she discovered she had no brown sugar.

"Sophie, will you run into Mrs. Cochran's and ask if we can borrow a cup of brown sugar?"

"Do I have to?"

"You love going to Mrs. Cochran's."

"No, I don't."

"You *used* to love it, then. What's happened?"

"Nothing. I'm too big to go there now, that's all."

Mum sighed and made a face. "Then I'm asking you to go in now, please, as a favor. I need the sugar."

I didn't see how I could get out of it. "All right. Where's the cup?"

I walked out the door and along the footpath. I hoped Mrs. Cochran was not home, but

I knew she'd be there. If I went on further, to Mr. Spooner at number 19, Mum would find out and ask more questions. I had to go to Mrs. Cochran's.

I opened the gate, went up the path and knocked on the front door.

Mrs. Cochran's whole face smiled at me. "Sophie! How lovely! Come in."

"I've only come for some brown sugar."

"And you came to the front door, too. We used to know each other better than that."

We walked down the passage, and it was cold and dark until we came to the kitchen. Mrs. Cochran measured out the sugar. "You haven't been here since that day," she said.

Which day? I stared at her, red-faced. "I've been busy."

"Of course. But you've got time now for afternoon tea?"

"I'm sorry, Mum's waiting for the sugar." It

was good to be able to tell the truth. "She's making fudge pudding."

Mrs. Cochran kneeled down and patted poor old Watson. He was on the floor, looking really saggy. "But you'll come again, won't you? Come and tell me about the new kitten—come soon."

"Thank you," I said. But I didn't say I'd go back another day. Through the back door, The Wild was singing out to me. I wanted to get lost in the long grass and listen to the air buzzing around my head. The Wild grew its own way and didn't need me.

There were biscuits in the oven. I felt mean that I wasn't staying to have one. But I *did* have a stomach ache. I really did.

Tangles gave up his box and slept on the end of my bed, just like Ginger did.

Dad said cats should go out at night, and Mum said my quilt would be full of fleas, but one night I heard them agree to let the animal sleep where it liked, if it kept me happy.

People say cats like houses better than people. I knew Tangles liked *me,* even if he thought I was another cat and not a girl. I didn't care if he thought I was a cat or a house or a tree or a rubbish bin. He *liked* me. He was my friend and my clock and my electric blanket.

I began to forget the time when there was no warm lump around my ankles.

For a while, friends came around to see the kitten. They dangled toy mice on strings and said things like: "Lucky you!"

Lucky, perhaps, but hidden inside me was the thought that Tangles was not really mine. He was Mrs. Cochran's too, because I'd taken Mrs. Cochran's money. The thought sat there like a blot you couldn't rub out. It wouldn't go away.

When Tangles grew bigger, mostly only Carla came to visit. She lay on the spare bed and talked about her stories. She was writing one about a girl who met a bad man in the street.

"I keep forgetting what I've written," she said. "I have to go back all the time and check my facts."

"But I thought you'd made it up."

"I have."

"Then it's easy. You don't have to check any facts."

Carla sat up and looked at me, as if she hadn't heard what I was saying. "Of course I do. I have to check my own facts—to be sure it makes sense."

She wanted me to understand. "It's like telling a lie, I suppose. I mean, if you tell the truth, you don't have to remember what you've said. But if you make something up, you have to remember and keep on saying the same thing, or you get caught out."

I heaved a great thick sigh and turned my back.

"So what!"

"Sorry!" said Carla. "I thought you knew all this."

"Why should I?" I felt as if the floor was rocking under my feet. "I don't need it."

"All right, then, if you're so cranky…"

"I'm not cranky. It's boring, that's all."

Her cheeks were pink. She stood up and walked towards the door.

I didn't want her to go. One thing Carla never was and that's boring. "Guess what?" I said. "Yesterday was Mum's birthday, and Dad gave her a chair."

She turned back and tried to smile. "That's a funny present."

"She didn't really want one, but she's already mad about it. She sat in it all night. It's gold velvet."

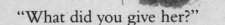

"What did you give her?"

"A lily. Pene Schmidt's father grows them. She sold me one, cheap."

"How much?"

"Three dollars."

"Three dollars! For a flower?"

"It's a growing one. They cost more than that in the shops."

Carla opened her eyes wide, as if she might understand better with her eyes open. "Did she like it?"

"Oh, yes! It's on the mantelpiece in the sitting room, where Tangles hasn't been yet. Pene's all right, when you get to know her."

"Where *is* Tangles, anyway?" asked Carla.

I called him, and he didn't come. "He was here a minute ago." I went into the kitchen and he wasn't there. I called out the window, but there was a sparrow on the lawn, and I knew it wouldn't be there if Tangles was in the yard.

The only other place was the sitting room. The door was open and I heard a grating sound. "Hey, Carla!" I yelled.

Tangles was sitting on the carpet with his

claws clinging to the side of Mum's new chair. I rushed in and grabbed him. There were scratch-marks down the velvet.

"What'll I do?" I wailed.

"Teach him a lesson," said Carla. "And quick—get a brush or something."

"That won't do it." I rubbed the scratched part with my fingers. "The threads are all pulled."

Carla ran her fingers across the marks. "It *is* rather rough."

"Oh, what'll I do?" I felt like howling.

Carla smoothed the velvet and stretched the cover into shape. "Look, it isn't *that* bad. Just make sure you tell your mother before she sees it."

I wasn't looking forward to that.

"Don't look so sick," said Carla. "She won't eat you."

"I've got this pain," I said. I didn't tell her I'd had it for weeks. Sometimes I thought I was imagining it. "But don't worry, I'll tell her."

As soon as Mum came home, I said: "Something awful has happened." And I told her about the chair. She and Tom and I went into the sitting room to look at it. Mum felt the scratchy velvet. "Well, it could be worse."

"Sorry," I said.

She put an arm around my shoulder. "Never mind, Sophie. We'll just have to train him better."

And keep the sitting-room door shut, I thought.

Mum picked the lily off the mantelpiece and carried it into the kitchen. "Let's have this in here, where we can enjoy it."

"Glad you like it," I said.

I'll never understand mothers. They fly off the handle about nothing, and when you expect them to go bananas they act as if they really love you. I thought my pain would go after this, but it didn't.

SIX

IT WAS A SUNNY SATURDAY. I was sitting on the back doorstep, hoping Carla would come around. She'd gone somewhere else every day after school that week.

Tangles was messing up my shoelaces. Dad was cooking bacon, and the smell poured out through the window. Saturdays like this feel yellow, after the grey school week. Everything was lazy and late, and nobody was making a noise.

That is, until a man called Mr. Thorne

arrived. He came in the back gate and saw me sitting there with my shoelaces undone. He had a cross look on his face, and I didn't smile.

"Is this number 14?"

The number was on the gate. So I just looked at him, to see what was coming next.

"I hear you've got a fantail."

"Not me, my brother."

He sucked in his cheeks, like our teacher before he yells at someone. I bet Mr. Thorne's a teacher. But he didn't yell at me then; he swallowed the yells. "Is your brother home?"

"He's in bed."

I don't think he liked that much.

"Could I see the pigeons, then?"

"I'll get Mum," I said. I picked up Tangles and went into the house. Mum was reading the newspaper. She hates people talking to her when she's reading Saturday's paper and she *really* hates it when people come to the door.

"There's a man here, Mum. He wants to see the pigeons."

"What for?"

"*I* don't know. He asked for Tom."

Mum went out to see the man. He nodded to her and said his name was Thorne, from Servetus Street. "I heard your son had a fantail."

"Yes."

"Could I see it?"

"Is he selling it?" asked Mum.

"I certainly hope not. How long has he had it?"

They walked under the clothesline. It was full

of washing. Every Saturday the washing's out and the pigeons are in. Mum knows how to dodge the washing, but the towels slapped Mr. Thorne in the face.

He flung a towel out of the way and took quick steps to the coop. "I knew it! That's my fantail!"

Mum's face was the color of a glass of milk. "But…it was a present…someone gave this bird to our son."

"It's *my* bird. I know it."

I ran inside and told Tom. "Quick, get up!" I shook him. "A man says you've got his fantail."

Tom's earphones made him look as if he was wired to the bed. He took them off and swore.

"It's not *my* fault, Tom. Come and tell him where you got it."

Tom crawled out of bed like an old man. He pulled on his tracksuit and clumped down the passage. "What the hell's going on?"

"It's all right," I said. "Just tell him where you got it."

Dad called out that the bacon was cooked, and if nobody came to eat it soon, they weren't getting any.

Tom muttered, "Hold it, Dad," and pushed open the back door with his foot. He saw Mr. Thorne and Mum standing beside the coop. Mr. Thorne had the white fantail on his arm.

"Where did you get this bird, son?" asked Mr. Thorne.

"A friend. It was a present."

"Four weeks ago?"

Tom nodded. "About that."

"Do you know where I live, son?"

"Haven't got a clue."

"Don't be rude, Tom," said Mum. She was starting to look really sick.

Mr. Thorne glared at Tom. "Are you sure?"

Tom glared back. "Are you saying I pinched the bird or something?" Then it hit him. "Bloody Billy! That's what happened! Billy pinched the fantail!"

Mum stuttered and stammered and said she was sorry about all this. Tom's face was red, and he kept on swearing and blaming Billy for everything.

"Take the thing! I don't want it! I never wanted it!"

Mr. Thorne said he'd take his bird and was prepared to forget the whole nasty incident. Mum said "Thank you," and Tom said "Thank you," but he said he wouldn't be forgetting what that stupid little creep had done to him. "All Billy ever did was get me into trouble."

None of us was hungry when we went in to eat our bacon. Mum didn't want any, and Tom said he'd kill Billy if he ever came around again.

"But Tom, he did it for you," I said.

"A thief's a thief, Sophie," said Tom.

I didn't say another word.

Mum said Billy had made a bad mistake, and Dad took off his chef's hat and said in future we could all cook our own bacon. Mum said this wasn't the time for clever talk, and suddenly they all stopped talking and our yellow Saturday had turned black.

I knew Billy would come around sometime that day. He'd bob up with a grin on his face and let the other kids knock him about. But this time Tom would blast him to bits.

I took Tangles out on the steps again, but I kept thinking about Billy. He'd done a really big thing for Tom. I'd feel warm inside if someone did that for me. But Tom was mad at Billy.

I told Mum I was going to get leaves for the last three silkworms. When she saw I was getting out my bike, she said: "What's wrong with Mrs. Cochran's place?" I said the leaves were better on the tree near Stringers Lane and rode off before she could say that was a pretty crummy answer.

I rode to Billy's house. There was a car without wheels in the driveway, and no flowers in the garden. I rang the bell, and a small, thin man opened the door. I knew he was Mr. Winks, because he looked like a squeezed-out Billy.

"Is Billy home?"

"Billy's out," he said. "He's gone to his friend Tom's place."

"No!" I cried.

"Don't worry, little girl. He'll be home for lunch."

"Oh, I'm not worried," I said. "Well, yes I

am, but I'd better go, thank you."

Mr. Winks smiled a dried-walnut sort of smile. "D'you know Billy, do you?"

"Yes."

"You'll often find him at Tom Brooker's place—such good friends, they are."

I started back towards the gate. Mr. Winks called after me. "D'you know where they live, do you?"

I waved to him and rode away. Poor Billy! He didn't know what was going to happen to him. Maybe he'd called in at the corner store on the way. I rode past it, but his bike wasn't there. I rode home faster than ever before. I had to stop Billy from seeing the hate on Tom's face.

When I turned the corner, Billy was crossing the road to our house. I yelled out to him, but he didn't hear. I pedaled harder and harder and kept on yelling. Billy got off his bike and opened our gate. I nearly burst my lungs, and then at last Billy turned and looked back. "What's wrong?" he said.

"Don't go in, Billy," I gasped. "Tom's a bit mad."

Billy grinned. "I don't mind."

"Billy, don't go in. He's found out where the fantail came from. There's been a bit of trouble, but it'll be all right if you just stay away for a while."

Billy went small and jumpy, like a mouse. "What'll I tell my dad?"

"I don't know." I hadn't chased him around Cattlesea to tell him that. "I just want you to stay away from here for a while."

"What...what did Tom say?"

"He's...um...sorry."

"Is that all?"

"Well, he's a bit mad, but he'll get over it. I mean, you did it for him."

Billy started to shake. "What'll I do? How can I tell my dad?"

"I don't know. But I know one thing, Billy. You can't make up a story about it. It'll only get worse if you do. Tell him what happened now, when you get home."

"I can't," said Billy. "He'll kill me."

"He won't, you know." I sounded like an old aunt. "Look, Billy, someone's going to come out that gate soon, so you'd better get going."

He stared at the footpath. "Thanks."

I started to say "Don't thank me," but I just watched as he rode away.

There was a flat feeling when I walked into the house. Mum said: "Where are the mulberry leaves?" and I said: "Oh! I forgot them."

She looked at me, as if I wasn't me anymore.

"Well, actually," I said—and I took a long time to say "*ac*…*tu*…*ally*"—"I ran into Billy on the way and I told him not to come here today. And then I forgot the leaves."

Mum smiled sadly at me. "I can understand that…Poor old Billy."

Tom was in his room with the music very loud. Mum pointed down the passage and said we'd better not mention this subject again. Tom had agreed not to say anything to anyone, provided he didn't have to talk to Billy anymore.

"But that's not fair. He did it for Tom."

"He's made it very difficult for Tom, too. What's Tom going to tell Steve and the others about the fantail?"

I hadn't thought about that.

"People should think a bit about what's right and wrong before they just take things," said Mum.

I stood there and felt she could see right through me. "You don't have to tell me," I said, a bit too loudly.

I was hot and sweaty all over. I went outside to find Tangles. He was asleep on the veranda, with his head tucked between his paws. I knew it was going to rain. It always rains when Tangles sleeps like that. Clouds like cauliflowers were coming closer, so I picked him up and went inside.

I lay on my bed. Dad looked in and said it was nearly lunchtime and I still hadn't had any breakfast, and I said I had a pain in my stomach. I couldn't eat anything. He said I did look pale, and suddenly the pain was so bad that I couldn't lie still on the bed. Mum and Dad put me in the car and took me to the doctor, and it was all so quick that I can't remember what happened, except that I didn't say good-bye to Tangles.

SEVEN

WHEN I WOKE UP, there was a stiff, heavy feeling in my side. It was like a brick on my stomach. I couldn't move. I opened my eyes. Mum said: "She's awake."

Someone said: "It's nine o'clock," and the lights were on, so I knew it was night. Mum said: "Poor Sophie, we didn't know what was wrong...all this time." I closed my eyes, and then it was morning.

Dad was there, not Mum, and he was wearing his Mickey Mouse hat with ears. The room was white, and the brick still sat on my stomach. Dad said: "You've had your appendix out, remember?"

I said: "Why?" My voice was croaky. "Why did I have them out?"

And he said: "Because it was in a really bad way. They only just got it in time."

"Then I'm glad they've gone."

"Who? Who's gone?" He thought I was having those hallucinations people have after operations. But I knew exactly what I was saying. "My appendix," I said.

"It's an *it*, silly." He stroked my head.

I said: "Where's Tangles?"

"He's all right. He's at home. He misses you."

"I'll be home in a minute," I croaked. But I wasn't home for three more days.

When I opened my eyes, Dad was gone, and

a nurse was holding my wrist and looking at her watch and saying things like: "You look better this afternoon."

"What time is it?" I asked, when I didn't know what day it was. "Where is everybody?" The brick was still there, but I wanted a big dinner and someone to talk to.

"You *are* better, aren't you!" said the nurse, and nodded and put her watch back in her pocket.

I thought: "There's nothing to do. I can't stay here much longer," when Tom walked in the door.

"G'day," he said. He looked around the ward and saw I was alone. Two other beds had screens around them. "What got into you?"

"What's gone out of me, you mean!" I grinned at him.

"You sound okay to me." He came and stood beside the bed.

"Haven't you been home yet?" I asked.

"Yes. Why?"

"You've still got your bag with you."

He put a finger to his mouth. "Shh." He went back and shut the door. Then he put the bag on the bed. He reached in and lifted Tangles onto the blanket.

"Tom!" I screeched. I laughed and the brick pulled on my stitches.

Tom grinned, pleased with himself. I held Tangles against my face.

"Of course, he didn't want to come," said Tom. "I had a dreadful job talking him into it."

I thought I could hear Tangles purring.

"He's had such a good time without you."

"Doing what?" I could definitely hear Tangles purring.

Tom sat on the end of the bed. "Well, he won't eat his dinner and he pees in the kitchen and he keeps us awake half the night howling."

I held Tangles away from me and looked into his four o'clock eyes. "How are the pigeons?" I asked.

"Fine, fine. I saw Billy yesterday."

"Oh!" I didn't say anything.

"He got a helluva hiding over the fantail."

"Who from?"

"From his father."

I stared at the neat, white bed cover. Poor Billy!

"He owned up to him," said Tom. "Pretty gutsy, eh?"

I nodded and pressed my face into Tangles' soft, black fur.

There was a knock on the door, and the handle turned. Tom jumped off the bed. I bundled Tangles under the sheet.

The door opened, and Carla stood there. "Hi! What's so funny?" She stared at the bump in the bed.

"Shut the door," said Tom.

"Don't say a thing," I said. "It's Tangles."

"I don't believe you." She looked at the empty bed and then at Tom. You could see her working out how Tangles got there. "Well, that's great, but I'm glad you don't have a dog as well."

Just then, the doorhandle turned again and a nurse walked in. "Everything all right here?"

Tom's face was red. I didn't worry about mine, because in hospital you're sick if it's red and you're sick if it's white. But I held my hand over the bump in the bed.

"I wondered why the door was shut," said the nurse.

"It…it's all right," I said. "My friend just came in."

She nodded. "Then I'll leave the door open."

Tom blew through his teeth. "Phew!"

I laughed. "Thank you for bringing him in." Tangles licked my wrist under the sheet and didn't want to leave.

"They'll kill me for bringing germs into this place," said Tom. "But one more thing." He reached into a pocket of the bag. "I've been feeding your silkworms, and Mrs. Cochran made you this." It was a posy of pink rosebuds. "And she asked if Tangles could come to her place."

"What do you mean?" The day of the fair

came rushing back at me. This was what I'd dreaded, ever since that day.

"Don't ask me," said Tom. "That's what she said."

"She's got Watson."

"He's too old."

The worst thing that could happen was happening now. I couldn't speak. I felt hollow inside. Empty. Alone.

"Are you all right, Sophie?" asked Carla. Up till then, she hadn't said much.

I swallowed. "It's just these stitches in my side."

Her face had the calm look, but she frowned. "I'm sorry. You *said* you had a pain...and I didn't come around."

"Don't worry. Nothing's your fault."

"Then it's all right now." She smiled, as if *she*

was forgiven. "I'll come as soon as you're home again."

Tom kept looking at the door. Footsteps sounded up and down the corridor. "I've had just about enough of this," he said. "I'm off." And he whisked Tangles away in his bag.

EIGHT

I DIDN'T SLEEP much that night.

Mum came to collect me in the morning, but she wasn't happy. While she put my clothes in a bag, she kept stopping, as if she was going to say something. Then she'd bite her lip and stuff another thing in the bag. I couldn't work out what was wrong.

I walked along the hospital corridor with my right knee nearly touching my chin.

"Try to walk tall," said the nurse.

I gritted my teeth and limped along the shiny

floor. Finally I asked: "Did you bring Tangles?"

Mum's cheeks had that milky look. "I've been trying to tell you. Tangles has gone."

"Gone?"

"He disappeared last night. He didn't come when we called him for dinner."

"Has Mrs. Cochran taken him?"

Mum stared straight ahead, as if she wasn't seeing anything. "Mrs. Cochran?" she mumbled. "Why?"

I didn't know what to say.

The nurse pretended not to hear.

"Have you looked for him?" I asked after a while.

"Of course we have. We've been everywhere. We've asked all round the neighborhood. We've hardly had any sleep." She put a hand on my shoulder. "But don't worry, Sophie. We'll find him."

"Did you…did you look on the road?" I could hardly get the words out.

Mum shook her head. "Sophie, *don't worry*. We…we would have heard."

The nurse took the bag from Mum. The corridor seemed longer and longer. I was going home, and Tangles wasn't there.

"Do try to straighten that leg," said the nurse.

Mum looked as if she'd had an operation too.

The nurse opened the door. The sun was bright in my eyes. I blinked.

Then I saw him. He was sitting under a tree across the hospital driveway; sitting, watching the door.

"Tangles!"

He flashed across the drive and jumped into my arms. "Ouch!"

"Goodness me! Careful!" cried the nurse. "Oh, dear! Are you all right?"

It did hurt…and it didn't. Nothing could really hurt you when your cat had walked all night to find you.

I held Tangles and looked at Mum. Her lip was twitching and I knew she'd been through one of the worst nights of her life.

"Sorry, Mum," I said.

She held her head up, so her nose wouldn't drip, and sniffed and said she was so happy she could sing.

Back home, Mum said: "Now, you sit here in the sun, and I'll get us some lunch."

I sat on the banana lounge on the back lawn and looked at the sports pages. I saw that it was Wednesday and knew that Mum had taken a day off work to be with me. How could you whine about a mum like that?

It should have been a golden day. Sun touched my skin, and the air was still, but fear stopped the sun from warming me. I couldn't run from it any longer. Mrs. Cochran was there next door, and she wanted Tangles.

Mum came out with cheese sandwiches and iced coffee and said I had another five days off school. Five days with Tangles was a holiday; without him, it would be a lifetime.

I took a bite of a sandwich. Tangles crept along the top of Mrs. Cochran's fence, and there was no sound from next door. "Where's Watson?" I asked.

"I was in there with Mrs. Cochran this morning," said Mum. She didn't answer my question.

"Well?"

"She had Watson put to sleep yesterday."

"Why?"

"He just grew old. We knew that. There was nothing more they could do."

I suppose I thought poor old Watson would always be there. "What's going to happen, then?"

"Mrs. Cochran will be lonely for a while and then perhaps she'll get another dog."

"Perhaps she will."

"You could go and say hello sometime tomorrow."

I swallowed. "Maybe." Maybe I would, maybe I wouldn't. What about Tangles? "It's cold out here," I said.

Mum stared, but said nothing. "You'd better go inside, then."

"Yes, I think I will."

It was cool inside, but I didn't care. My room

closed around me. What could I say to Mrs. Cochran now Watson had gone? Her house was empty. No panting black sack on the floor, no bowl to fill each evening. I knew what it was like, having an empty bowl by the door. What could I say to her? "Sorry" was not enough. People said "Sorry" about anything… *Sorry I spilled my drink on your carpet…sorry I stepped on your toe…sorry I didn't write.*

In a corner of my room, the first moths were whirring their wings, before they laid eggs for next year's silkworms. The last silkworm had begun to spin in a corner of the box. Gold cocoons hung along the sides. I'd been too lazy to spin the silk. Every year I was going to make a scarf, and I never did. Pene Schmidt put me off when she said you needed three thousand silkworms to get a kilogram of silk. Someone always spoils things. But one good thing—mulberry leaf days were over. I didn't have to feed the moths. Soon they'd be lying stiff in their boxes, with eggs like little seeds beside them.

Tangles slunk into the room and brushed against my legs. He settled in a lump across my toes and began to purr. It was like a "Thank you for having me."

Through my window, I could see the fence and Mrs. Cochran's roof. It was so quiet. Mrs. Cochran was in there, I knew. I wondered what she was doing. Had anyone made her a posy or said nice things? She would be sitting in the kitchen, prodding her hair back into her bun, sitting, thinking, by herself. Tangles went on purring.

I heard Tom crashing up the passage. He called out "Hello, No-appendage! See you later!" and crashed out again. In our house, we had Mum and Dad and Tom and Tangles—the pigeons, even—and Mrs. Cochran had nothing.

I picked up Tangles and held him on my lap. He was still purring.

The room filled with shadows. Mum said why didn't I come out and watch the TV. "You can't sit there in the dark all afternoon."

I didn't say anything.

"Are you all right, Sophie?"

"Yes."

"Then why don't I go and get a video?"

"No, thanks. Carla's coming after school." I sat, staring down at Tangles, wishing Mum would go away.

She walked to the door. I heard her sigh, as if she didn't know what to do with me. She thought the operation would fix everything. But there were some things no doctor could fix.

In the night, things stand out in your mind. They jump at you, out of the dark. First, there was Carla, telling me about truth and lies. Then there was Tangles with a five-dollar price tag, running through the streets to find me in the hospital. There was Mrs. Cochran, calling him down from the tree. She kept on calling. She knew about the money. That's why she was asking for Tangles.

I lay awake all night. My cheek made a hot patch on the pillow. The hours clicked over, minute by minute, and slowly my mind was made up.

NINE

I DRESSED AS soon as I heard the radio in
the kitchen. My eyes were puffy. My legs
ached, and the brick was still there.

"Did you sleep well?" asked Mum, even
though she saw my red eyes and gluey hair.

"I don't want any breakfast," I said. "I'm
going in to see Mrs. Cochran."

Dad came into the kitchen, shiny from his
shower. "What-ho! No school and Sophie's up
already."

"She's going to see Mrs. Cochran," said Mum. She smiled.

"Before breakfast?" said Dad.

I nodded. Tangles stayed close, because he knew I was going somewhere. I bent down and picked him up. "I'm taking Tangles."

I went out quickly, before I changed my mind. Between our door and Mrs. Cochran's gate, I told myself that it wouldn't kill me. *I won't die. Tangles won't die.* Then what's the worst thing that could happen? I might never see Tangles again. But he'll be next door. I can go in anytime. Still, he won't be mine. I'll be a visitor. Do I have to *own* him? Yes, I do. It's special, having your own cat.

My feet slowed almost to a stop. Tangles' ears brushed against my chin. His eight o'clock eyes looked into mine. I pushed open the gate.

Mrs. Cochran was watering the front garden. "Ah! Sophie! Good, you've come." She turned off the tap and untied her apron. She waved it in the air. "Come inside, come on."

Her kitchen smelled of warm crumbs. She put a saucepan of milk on the stove. "Cocoa?"

I sat on a chair with Tangles on my lap. I started to say I was sorry about Watson, but I just went mumble-mumble. Mrs. Cochran smiled. "Watson had a good life." Her voice grew softer. "But I'll miss him."

There was an empty space where Watson used to lie.

Mrs. Cochran stroked Tangles. "He's just what I need." She gave me a long look.

Mumble-mumble-mumble. "I brought him for you." I stood up and held him out to her. She turned to the stove, and I was left holding Tangles.

I stared at her back, while she stirred the cocoa.

"Put him down, if you like," she said. "He

might catch a mouse or two. The house is full of them."

Tangles stretched and sniffed around the walls. He prodded at a crack above the floorboards and did the mouse-pounce around the kitchen. "He's practicing," said Mrs. Cochran. "That'll be a mousehole there. Good cat, Tangles. I've been wanting to borrow you for this."

Borrow! The word echoed in my mind.

"And I've got something to tell you, Sophie."

We sat at the table, drinking cocoa. Tangles crouched in the center of the room, watching the hole.

I waited.

"I once knew a girl who pinched a book from the newsagent's," said

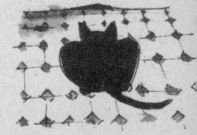

Mrs. Cochran. "She was only seven at the time, but she wanted that book. It had a kitten on the cover. Even today, she can still see the cover. *Marietta's Gift,* it was called. The girl never liked the book. She read it under the blankets one night, and it was a good book, but she never liked it. She didn't know what to do with it. She hid it under her bed, until one day, when no one was looking, she pushed it into one of those bags people leave at the gate. She felt better when it had gone, but only a bit better. She tried to forget the book, but she never could. It never truly went away."

I said nothing. Mrs. Cochran sat looking at me. There was a sudden swish under our feet and Tangles flashed across the room. He stopped, with a mouse between his paws. Mrs. Cochran clapped her hands. "He's done it!" She opened the door. "Good fellow, Tangles. Take it outside now."

She put her hand under my elbow. "We'll go too."

Tangles streaked ahead and disappeared into the long grass.

The Wild was wet with dew. It left damp patches on the legs of my jeans. New poppies were opening like red crepe paper. The sun made stripes in the grass, and the air smelled of honey jumbles.

The Wild grows its own way and won't stop for anyone. People aren't like that. I stood there and remembered why I had come.

"Do…do you want to keep him?" I said. "Tangles, I mean."

"He would be useful, now and then. Could you bring him in again?"

"He…he's really yours, if you want him."

Mrs. Cochran shook her head, until the hair fell out of her bun. "Do you know, Sophie, I've never told a soul that story before." She tapped her chest. "It's been in here all this time."

I knew then that she was the girl. And she knew *I* was the girl, too. I didn't ask how she knew. She'd always known. When I lifted my head, her eyes were warm and forgiving. Her arms went around me, and it felt good to be there.

"I'll bring Tangles in tomorrow," I said. "We can share."

"Thank you, Sophie. I feel much better now."

"Me too."

I walked in our door with Tangles across my shoulders, the way I used to carry Ginger. It felt comfortable and right now, having Tangles.

Mum was reading a book on glazes.

"Aren't you going to work today?" I asked.

"I'm having a few days off, like you. How was Mrs. Cochran?"

"Good," I said. "Very good."

"I'm glad you went." Mum was groping, searching for signs that I was over the grumps.

"Thanks for staying home," I said. I smiled at her, and she smiled, and it was like when you've been to the dentist and nothing needed doing.

"I'm starving," I said. I ate a muffin with heaps of honey and slept for I don't know how long.

The afternoon was like another day. It might have been Thursday or Friday. The first thing I saw, when I looked out the window, was Billy's bicycle propped against our garage.

I went onto the veranda.

"Hi, Sis," called Tom. His bicycle was upside-down on the lawn. "Billy came round to fix my puncture."

"Can't you do it yourself?"

"Yeah, but Billy's better at it. Besides, can't you see I'm busy?" He was winding a bit of old carpet around a broomstick. Billy was squatting there, holding the bicycle tube in a bucket of water. He looked up at me and grinned.

"Hi, Billy," I said, like I always did.

I walked down to them. "Hey, Tom, it's a scratching pole!"

"'Course it is. And make sure that cat jolly well uses it." He hammered the broomstick into a wooden block. "I tried to finish it while you were in hospital, but you came home too soon."

"*Thanks very much,*" I said. I'd been there quite long enough.

Billy said he'd found the puncture and he'd have it fixed in two minutes. Tom said, "Good on you, Billy," and I could see I wasn't needed.

Tangles followed me up the steps to the house. I didn't walk, I danced. The air carried me. When I opened the door, it was like bringing Tangles home for the first time, only better.